P9-ECN-182

WITHDRAWN

The Big Lie

by Fran Manushkin
illustrated by Tammie Lyon

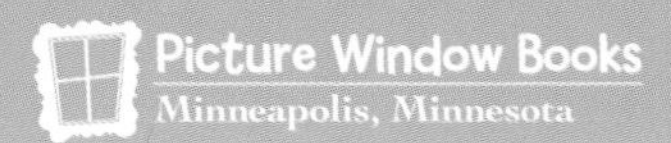

Katie Woo is published by Picture Window Books
A Capstone Imprint
151 Good Counsel Drive, P.O. Box 669
Mankato, MN 56002
www.capstonepub.com

Library of Congress Cataloging-in-Publication Data
Manushkin, Fran.
The big lie / by Fran Manushkin; illustrated by Tammie Lyon.
p. cm. — (Katie Woo)
ISBN 978-1-4048-5497-0 (library binding)
ISBN 978-1-4048-6055-1 (softcover)
[1. Honesty—Fiction. 2. Schools—Fiction. 3. Chinese Americans—Fiction.]
I. Lyon, Tammie, ill. II. Title.
PZ7.M3195Bi 2010
[E]—dc22 2009001851

Summary: When Jake loses his brand new airplane toy, Katie Woo lies and says that she does not know where it is.

Creative Director: Heather Kindseth
Graphic Designer: Emily Harris

Photo Credits
Fran Manushkin, pg. 26
Tammie Lyon, pg. 26

Printed in the United States of America in Stevens Point, Wisconsin.
052010
005814R

Table of Contents

Chapter 1

The Missing Plane

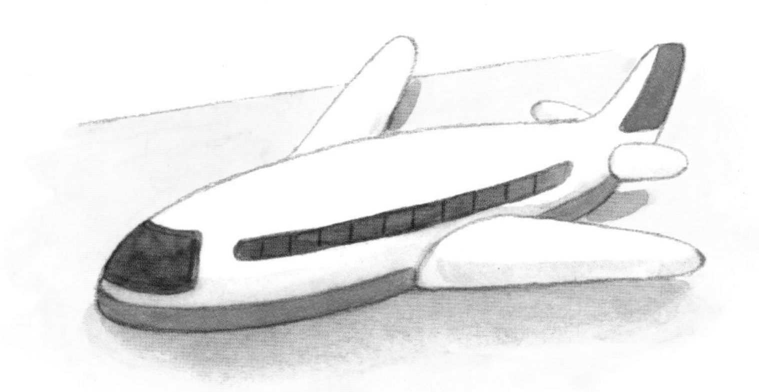

One day after recess, Miss Winkle told the class, "Jake has lost his toy airplane. Has anybody found it?"

Katie Woo shook her head no. So did her friends Pedro and JoJo and everyone else.

“My father gave me

the airplane yesterday,”

said Jake.

"It was a birthday present," he said.

"Maybe your plane flew away," said someone else.

"That is not funny," said Miss Winkle.

JoJo told Jake, "I saw you playing with your plane at recess. It's so neat! I hope you find it."

Miss Winkle asked again,

"Does anyone know where

Jake's airplane is?"

“I don’t,” Katie told Jake.

But she was lying.

Chapter 2

Katie's Bad Grab

Earlier that day during recess, Katie saw Jake running around with his airplane.

"I want to do that!" Katie told herself. "I wish that plane belonged to me."

When recess was almost
over, three fire trucks sped by.

While everyone was watching them and waving to the firefighters, Katie grabbed Jake's plane. She put it into her pocket.

Now Jake's plane was inside Katie's desk.

"I can't wait to play with it when I go home," Katie thought.

During art class, Katie said, "Maybe a kangaroo hopped over and put the airplane in her pouch."

"I don't think so," said Miss Winkle. "There are no kangaroos around here."

During spelling, Katie said, “Maybe the garbage man came and took Jake’s plane.”

“No way!” JoJo said. She shook her head. “I didn’t see any garbage trucks.”

Jake kept staring at the empty box that his airplane came in. The birthday ribbon was still on the box.

Jake looked like he was going to cry.

Katie didn't feel happy either.

When nobody was looking, she took something out of her desk and put it into her pocket.

Chapter 3

The Truth

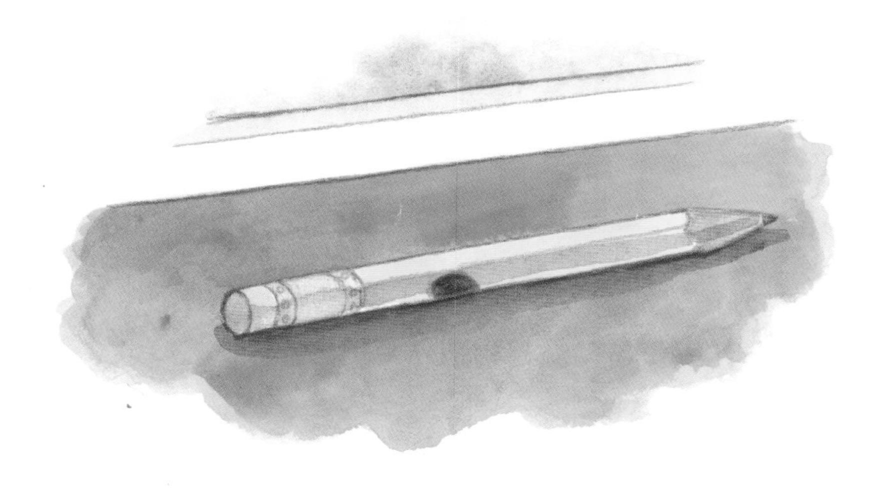

Katie walked to the window and began using the pencil sharpener.

All of a sudden, Katie yelled, “I see Jake’s plane. It’s by the window! It must have flown in during recess.”

Katie handed Jake the plane. She whispered, "That was a lie, Jake. I took your plane, and I am very sorry!"

At first, Jake was angry at Katie. Then he said, "I am glad you gave it back. I feel a lot better now."

"I do too!" Katie said.

And that was the truth.

About the Author

Fran Manushkin is the author of many popular picture books, including *How Mama Brought the Spring; Baby, Come Out!; Latkes and Applesauce: A Hanukkah Story;* and *The Tushy Book*. There is a real Katie Woo — she's Fran's great-niece — but she never gets in half the trouble of the Katie Woo in the books. Fran writes on her beloved Mac computer in New York City, without the help of her two naughty cats, Cookie and Goldy.

About the Illustrator

Tammie Lyon began her love for drawing at a young age while sitting at the kitchen table with her dad. She continued her love of art and eventually attended the Columbus College of Art and Design, where she earned a bachelors degree in fine art. After a brief career as a professional ballet dancer, she decided to devote herself full time to illustration. Today she lives with her husband, Lee, in Cincinnati, Ohio. Her dogs, Gus and Dudley, keep her company as she works in her studio.

Glossary

either (EE-thur or EYE-thur)—also

empty (EMP-tee)—nothing inside

garbage (GAR-bij)—things that are thrown away

recess (REE-sess)—a break from school

sharpener (SHARP-en-er)—an item that is used to make something sharper

Discussion Questions

1. Katie was jealous of Jake. She wanted his airplane for herself. Have you ever been jealous of someone?

2. Katie lied to Jake. Has anyone ever lied to you? How did it make you feel?

3. The teacher didn't find out that Katie took the plane. What do you think would have happened if the teacher found out?

Writing Prompts

1. Katie broke some rules in the story. Write down at least one rule she broke.

2. Katie said that a kangaroo might have taken the airplane. Draw a picture of a kangaroo with the plane, and write a sentence about your kangaroo.

3. Katie apologized for taking the plane. Pretend you need to apologize for something, and write a letter to say you're sorry.

Having Fun with Katie Woo

In this book, Katie Woo told a big lie. Everyone knows that lying is wrong. But with this game, you can tell lies and nobody will get hurt.

The Truth and Lies Game

Play this game with a group of friends or classmates.

1. Each player needs a piece of paper and a pen or pencil.

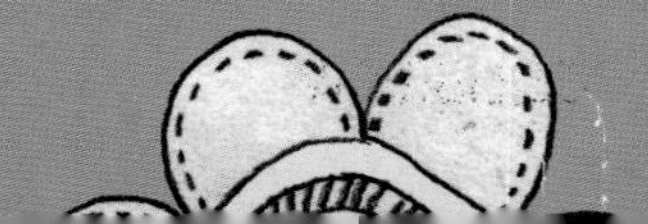

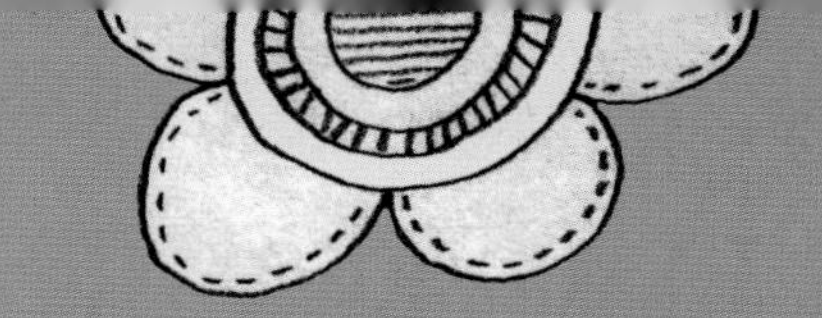

2. Each player writes down three items about themselves. You could share your favorite things, best vacations, or hobbies. But one thing should be true and two things should be lies.

3. Take turns reading your lists of three things. After all three items have been read, the group takes a vote on which item is true. When the vote is complete, the reader tells the group which one is true.

You're sure to learn lots of fun things about your friends.

FIND MORE:

Games & Puzzles
Heroes & Villains
Authors & Illustrators

www.CAPSTONEKIDS.com

STILL WANT MORE?

Find cool websites and more books like this one at www.FACTHOUND.com.
Just type in the BOOK ID: 9781404854970 and you're ready to go!